Hard Luck

A Straight To Gay Football MM Instalove Romance

(First Time for Everything Series)

By B.T. Haiyes

Copyright © 2022 B.T Haiyes.

All Rights Reserved.
Print Edition.
This is a work of pure fiction.
Names, places, business, characters and/or incidents mentioned in this book are either the product of the author's imagination, or are used in a fictitious manner.
Any resemblance to actual persons living or dead, actual events or places is purely coincidental.
No part of this book may be reproduced in any form or by any electronic or mechanical means, including information storage and retrieval systems, without written permission from the author, except for the use of brief quotations in a book review.
All rights not mentioned herein are reserved to the author.

Table of Contents

Chapter 1

CHASE

"Chase, get down!" I ducked down with a yelp, as my best friend tugged at my shoulder, dragging me behind the low shrubbery.

Crouching awkwardly, I stilled as I held my breath. Hidden behind a bush, I tried to stay as quiet as possible, even though I knew I would not be heard over the thunderous noise coming from the nightclub across the street.

"How much longer are we going to have to stay here?" I whispered through gritted teeth. When Tyler didn't answer, I lightly punched him in the shoulder to get his attention.

He cast an exasperated look over at me. "I know as much as you do right now."

"Yeah, but this was all your idea," I indicated the bush we were ducked behind. "By the time the waiters leave, the party is going to be long over."

I shifted my weight as I tried to get comfortable. But, I still kept my body taut, ready to spring into action if Tyler gave the word.

The sun had long since set, and it was late into the evening. And yet, there was still just enough streetlight for me to pick out the *Minnie's Food & Delivery*' signage on the side of the caterer van.

"Give me a second, I've got this," Tyler assured me, his eyes remaining pinned on the caterers across the road.

The food delivery personnel worked tirelessly, moving in and out of the nightclubs side door. They were ferrying a seemingly endless supply of champagne bottles into the bouncing club.

"Let's try and bribe the caterers. Worse that'll happen is that they don't let us through." I shifted again, trying to keep my weight off my bum left knee. "Or maybe we could try bribing the bouncers at the door again," I continued, as I brushed a touch of dirt off the other knee of my slacks.

Tyler's eyes never left the side door of the club. Especially now that two of the delivery staff were taking a cigarette break. "*Shh!* We have to stay quiet if we want this to work," Tyler told me, not noticing my rolling eyes.

I grunted a half-hearted acknowledgment, even though I thought Tyler's admonishment was ridiculous.

'Tyler really thinks we're going to be heard over that din?'

It was a wonder the club hadn't yet got hit by the cops citing a noise violation. You could hear the music all the way down two city blocks.

'I guess that's simply one of the many perks of being a play-off football team.' I thought to myself. *'You can turn up the music at the party of the year, and the city will turn a blind a eye.'*

Still, I couldn't quite shake off the feelings of annoyance at having traveled three hours to get here. And all the while I'd thought Tyler had actually gotten us invites into the Dashing Colonels football squads play-off celebration party.

Yet, as soon as we'd arrived, it soon became obvious that Tyler's invite was less of an invite, and more of a plan to gate-crash the party.

Plus, to add insult to injury, it seemed like we were about to spend an entire wasted Saturday night hiding behind this bush.

"Right, I've got it," Tyler said, and he turned to give me a mischievous smile. I eyed him cautiously as he continued. "I have an idea, but we're going to need to move fast. So, stay low."

I didn't bother to keep the sarcasm from flavoring my words. "You know I am wearing dress shoes, right? If I'd known there'd be cardio involved, I'd have worn something else."

"Hey, I'm not happy about this either," Tyler indicated his velvet slip-ons, the ones he'd told me he'd spent nearly half a months pay check on. "You think I want to be running around in these beauties?" He cast a mournful look down at his brown velvet shoes. "But, it'll all be worth it once we're inside." Tyler re-affixed his attention on the caterer van.

"And how are we going to do that?" I asked, as I curiously watched Tyler straighten up out of his crouched position.

He tapped me on my shoulder, indicating that I stand up as well. "When I say *run*, you follow after me," Tyler told me as he began to move out from behind the shrub.

Completely non-plussed, I wordlessly followed. But, it took me a moment to realize what Tyler planned to do.

"Come on, you can't seriously think we'll get in through that side entrance..." Before I could finish my sentence, Tyler yelled.

"RUN!"

I didn't hesitate. Running as fast as I could, I tracked Tyler closely as we both sprinted across the road, mainlining for the side door.

The delivery staff barely had time to shout after us, before we managed to slip in through the door unimpeded.

But we didn't stop. Tyler and I continued to speed through the kitchen, skipping past one catering staff member after another, as we headed straight for the swinging doors that led into the nightclub.

As I kept pace with Tyler, my heart racing with adrenalin, one thought kept running through my mind.

'I can't believe that actually worked!'

Chapter 2

JAKE

I took a long slow sip from my champagne glass. Anything to distract myself from the inane conversation that I was somehow trapped in.

"...that's when I decided I simply had to have the butt implants done as well."

I made a non-committal *hum* sound, my eyes drifting away from the chattering woman, to scan the bouncing nightclub.

She placed a hand on my forearm, bringing my attention back to her, as she leaned in to whisper co-conspiratorially. "You can feel them if you like," she said, twisting her hips to thrust her butt at me. Her short thigh-high glittering dress hugged her body in all the right places. "I won't mind. They feel completely real". She clearly kept her body in great shape — breast, lip, and apparently butt implants aside.

And yet, she did nothing for me.

I have no idea why she thought I would want to grab her ass. Maybe my other football team mates were still into those women who threw themselves at pro-players. But those days were long behind me.

At the grand old age — by pro football standards — of 26 years old, I'd soon come to realize that a different girl every night wasn't what I wanted.

More than that, I'd long since figured out that I was less than straight. I was bi, for sure. And yet, relationship wise, I was always on the look out for a hard-muscled man to take to my bed.

But, life in the spotlight of a major football team meant I couldn't take any chance jumping into the gay dating scene. The last man I'd dated

— beyond the odd quick one night stand — was when I was 22 years old and still playing college football.

That relationship had ended disastrously. And I'd come dangerously close to being outed, all before my career had even started.

Ever since then, publicly, I'd only been seen dating an endless string of women. And those relationships had ended as fast as my discreet gay-dating-app hookups did.

'Once bitten, twice shy,' I thought to myself with a barely audible sigh.

The woman — *Katie? Lacy? I forget her name* — continued to shamelessly flirt with me, slowly dragging her hand up my forearm to rest it on my bicep.

"Damn," she said the word with a long wanton moan, "you must work out all the time. You're arms are so firm. Are you firm everywhere else too?" She didn't bother to hide how her eyes drifted down to my groin, before trailing her gaze back up my body to meet my eyes.

And with that, I was done feigning interest.

I'd only left the VIP section of the club to get a breather from the celebrations happening in there. The entire squad were taking full advantage of the facilities. And the raucous VIP area was filled with drinking and shouting as everyone yukked it up.

I, on the other hand, didn't feel much like celebrating. Sure, we'd won the play-off game and were through to the next round. But, my own performance as a running back was less than stellar.

Our captain and quarterback, Lou Howard, had told me to shrug it off and simply do better next game.

Still, I didn't feel I'd earned the right to celebrate as hard as the other guys on the team. So, I'd wandered away from the group into the crowd of club-goers and lingering Dashing Colonels fans.

And this woman — *Macy? Tracy? God, what is her name again?!* — had latched onto me the moment I'd left the exclusive cornered off VIP area.

With my free hand, I gently grasped her hand and removed it from my arm. I wasn't interested, and I certainly wasn't willing to play along for the sneaky tabloid paparazzi that were no doubt in here waiting to snap a picture.

"I'm going to go get a refill." I stopped her when she started to follow after me. "No, you stay here, I'll be right back," I said, not pausing to hear her reply. With a quick glance over my shoulder, I breathed a short sigh of relief, when I noticed she did not follow after me.

But, as I turned to face forward, I heard someone yell *'on your right!'* as they ran towards me. Brushing my shoulder, the slight man breezed past into the crowd with a short whoop of delight.

"What the hell?" I called after him, while I heard shouts of *'hey, you two!'* come from the direction he'd just run from.

Turning around to the shouts, another man ran right into me with an *'oof!'*, as he face-planted into my chest.

I noticed that this stranger barely came up to my shoulders, as he bounced off my six foot five inch frame.

Still, I barely felt it — I'd been rushed by guys 2 or 3 times heavier on the football field — but it seemed like the stranger felt the full force of my solid body.

The man rocked back from the recoil. Still, he managed to quickly mumble a *'sorry'* in my direction, while snapping his head around to look over his shoulder.

The movement threw the man off balance, and he began to topple over. So, in a swift move, I reached out to grasp his shoulders, steadying him from falling down flat on his ass.

The weight of my hands on his body made this stranger finally drag his eyes away from the men chasing him, and he turned his gaze to peer up at me.

And when our eyes met, I found myself transfixed by the most beautiful green eyes I'd ever seen.

Chapter 3

CHASE

It felt like I'd just run into a solid brick wall.

When my forehead bounced off the man's chest, that was embarrassing enough. But I was so distracted by the security guards giving chase, that I nearly tripped over my feet.

I didn't know what would be worse. Getting caught by the burly security, or getting into a fight with this huge man mountain.

Yet, instead of a fist to my face, all I felt were surprisingly gentle hands steadying me.

I peered up at the man. He had to have had at least a half-a-foot advantage over my five foot nine inches. Yet, instead of finding anger, I was surprised to be met by a crystal blue eyed look of concern.

He towered over me, with shoulders so broad, you couldn't even see past them. His jawline looked like it had been carved from marble, and it was covered in carefully trimmed stubble.

We stood like that for a long moment — standing entirely too close — with his hands on my shoulders. But we were soon interrupted, as the two security guards rushed in.

"I apologize, Mr. Goode." One of the guards addressed the blue-eyed stranger, before moving to grab my arm.

The stranger — *or rather, Mr. Goode* — dropped his hands from my shoulders, and moved to stop the security guard.

"What are you doing?"

"Apologies again, sir." The security guard actually sounded embarrassed at having to haul me off. "This guy and his friend snuck in via the kitchen entrance. A lapse in security like that will not happen again."

The security guards hand tightened around my bicep, as he started to tug me away.

"We didn't sneak in…" I began in protest, but my voice faded a little underneath the glare of the guard. "Okay, look. It's a funny story. Once you hear it from my friend, Ty…um." I wasn't going to land Tyler in it. If I had to go down, the least I could do was make sure Tyler's name didn't come up. "Ty-Reese. My friend Tyrese is around here somewhere." I made a show of looking around for Tyler, trying not to cringe at how obvious my lie sounded. "I'm sure we can clear this all up…"

Mr. Goode interrupted my rambling.

"He's with me."

My eyebrows rose at that, and I didn't bother hide my surprise that this stranger was covering for me.

And the two security guards appeared as equally surprised as I was.

"Are you sure, sir?" The second security guard asked. He was stood a little aways from me, no doubt ready to block my escape, if I managed to slip from the first guards grip.

Despite the obvious looks of skepticism swapped between the two guards, the first guard loosened his grip from my arm.

Mr. Goode moved to pat the guard on the shoulder. "I know you're just doing your job. So many people are trying to get into this party, it's gotta be hard work. But we need you guy's looking out for us," he continued, pointing between the two guards. "The team needs time to blow off steam, without hangers-on bothering us."

The first guard seemed to puff up his chest, a a genuine smile drawing itself across his features at the compliment. "Absolutely! The Dashing Colonels are going to go all the way this year. So, this is the least we can do." The security guard gave me a short nod. "Sorry about that. I believe we were mistaken earlier." There was a color to the mans tone that clearly indicated that he didn't believe that at all. Still, the guard turned back to regard Mr. Goode. "And if you need anything sir, my friend and I," he jutted a thumb over at his security guard partner, "you let us know. We're stood by the entrance."

Mr. Goode nodded with a charming smile. "Good to know. And, *Goode Luck*!" He said, with a chuckle.

I watched the exchange wordlessly, feeling lost when the two guards both laughed along with him. "Damn straight! *Goode Luck* at the next game, sir."

And with that, the guards both walked away.

I stood looking nonplussed, wondering what the hell had happened. Who was this Mr. Goode guy?

'And whats with all of that weird good lucking?' I thought to myself.

I didn't have time to mull over it for long, because Mr. Goode then addressed me with his hand outstretched. I took it.

"And what might your name be?"

"Chase. Chase Mason," I replied, confused as to where this was going. I then remembered my manners. "Thanks for getting those guards off my case," I shook his hand. His grip was tight, but not painfully so. As we loosened our grip, I continued. "I'm sorry about all of that. Mr. Goode, was it?" I queried.

The tall stranger laughed. "Mr. Goode? That's way too formal. Call me Jake. Jake Goode's my full name. But, don't tell me you didn't already know that."

I gave him a genuinely confused look. "I really don't."

Jake chuckled as he indicated the bouncing night club around us. "I mean, you're the one here at the team party. You really mean to tell me you don't know who I am?"

'Should I be recognizing this guy? Is he on the team?' I thought to myself. *'Damn it Tyler. If he was here, he'd know who this guy was.'*

As I racked my brain, trying to figure out who Jake was, I knew it was going to be hopeless.

I didn't follow football, or any sport really. Ever since high school, I was always much more at home working with computer code. And I would always steer clear of any jocks that crossed my path.

And all throughout college, my friend group was made up of people who didn't put much stock in any sports team.

Even my best friend Tyler, was more of a fair-weather football fan, than a die-hard sports addict.

But, Tyler had been closely following the Dashing Colonels more, as our states football team started to win games consistently. And with their recent winning streak, it was next to impossible to avoid some news bit on TV about how well the team was doing.

The whole reason Tyler and I even came to the party, was because Tyler had recently got it into his head to try and become a sports agent. And he wanted me along with him for support.

This trip was all about Tyler getting a chance to cozy up to the players and management on the Dashing Colonels, and begin making connections.

I on the other hand, didn't know any player on this team — besides the captain. And that's only because Tyler wouldn't shut the hell up about him.

So who on earth was stood in front of me?

I gave Jake a helpless shrug. "Should I?"

Jake looked at me curiously. "You really have no idea who I am?" He sounded almost impressed.

I shrugged again.

"So, you ran up into the party because?..." Jake let his question trail off.

"Well, my friend Ty...er, Ty-lone," I stumbled over my words. "I came with him, my friend Tylone."

Jake gave me another more ponderous look. "That's your friend *Tyrese*, from earlier?" He emphasized the name, clearly indicating that he wasn't buying it.

I nodded.

"I think he may have ran into me earlier." Jake scratched his chin.

"*That's sounds about right,*" I muttered under my breath, wondering what Tyler had gotten me into. "Anyway, thanks for the cover with those guys," I said out loud as I thumbed over my shoulder in the direction of the two security guards. "So, I should get going…"

"Wait up. You're going?" Jake rushed, his eyebrows raised. And I could have sworn he even looked a touch crestfallen.

'*What's that about?*' I thought to myself, as I nodded. "I need to find my friend." I made a show of glancing around the room, but found no hint of Tyler anywhere. Instead, the only person who caught my eye was a woman stood curiously nearby, her eyes affixed on Jake's back. "You know her?" I said, staring pointedly past Jake.

Jake glanced over his shoulder, then snapped his head back with a groan. "Damn it, I thought I shook her off," he said, rubbing a hand tiredly across his face. He then stilled, peering at me with a strange look. "You can help me out."

"Huh, *what*?"

"Yep," Jake brightened, a disarmingly charming smile broadening across his face. "Help me out with this, and we can call it even."

"Call what even?" I felt completely spun by the direction of the conversation. "Help you out with what again?"

"Just follow my lead," Jake moved to draped an arm around my shoulders, letting loose a much-too-loud laugh. He then made a show of talking even louder. Although who he was suddenly talking too, I had no clue. "I know, dude. It's great to see you again. You've gotta come meet the team."

It took me a second too long — coupled with the earnest pleading look on Jake's face — for me to catch on.

"Oh, of course?" I answered, more a question than a statement. I stumbled a little as I repeated myself, sounding a bit more sure this time. "Of course! The team! The football team!"

I cringed at my D-list level acting, but I'd been put on the spot.

Jake then began to guide us through the crowd, towards the roped off area of the club. We passed by the staring woman — who Jake studiously ignored as she tried to get his attention — as we continued our weirdly loud nonsensical conversation.

"I've heard great things about the team." I was ad-libbing, racking my brain for any kernel of football knowledge I'd managed to absorb in passing about the squad. "All of those winning games."

Jake burst out with fake laughter. "Seriously, Chase. Never change, dude. Never change."

We were now far enough away from the woman — and near enough to the VIP room — that I felt I'd now fulfilled my duty.

Daring a look over my shoulder, I noticed the groupie wander off in a huff, pushing her way aggressively through the crowd.

Turning back to Jake, I let him know the good news. "She's gone. I think she took the hint."

Expecting Jake to then immediately drop his arm from my shoulder, I was surprised as he continued to guide us both to the VIP section.

"That's awesome. Now, let's see about getting you a drink." Jake waved at the two unfamiliar security guards who stood watch at the entryway to the VIP area.

My eyes widened, when both guards merely nodded, as one of them moved to unhook the rope, and allow Jake through.

There were loud raucous sounds coming from the VIP entryway. "You actually want me to go in there with you?" I said, even while I continued to allow myself be led inside.

Jake's hand move from my shoulders to my upper back, as though he could sense my hint of nervousness. Yet strangely enough, Jake's palm felt comforting as it rested there.

"Don't worry, they're a great bunch of guys." Jake nodded to the security guards as we passed them. "And the drinks in there are better than out here too."

I was thinking of protesting, but I was actually a little curious to see what was happening in that exclusive section. Tyler had told me that Dashing Colonels parties were legendary.

Besides, I also wanted to get to know Jake a little better. What's more, maybe I could help Tyler get an in with the team and their coaching staff, by partying the night away with them.

'*What the hell*,' I thought to myself, and then said out loud. "Lead on Mr. Goode."

Chapter 4

JAKE

The VIP room was jam-packed with every single Dashing Colonels player on my team. And each player seemingly had at least two groupies hanging off their arms.

Even a few of the so-called *'happily married'* players on my team, were playing the field in here. Almost as well as they'd played on the actual football field.

But I wasn't into any of it. I'd long since lost a taste for fans who only wanted something from me just because I was on the Dashing Colonels squad.

Which was why I wanted to spend more time with Chase.

It's been a long time since someone hadn't recognized me, or immediately wanted something out of me.

And it didn't hurt that Chase was very easy on the eyes too.

So, Chase and I sat in one of the corner booths, with a perfect wide-scope view of the action going on around us. And Chase looked positively star-struck by some of the movie stars in the room.

And as I eased back into my seat, I took advantage of Chase's distracted celebrity-gazing, to let my eyes rake over him.

Chase was wearing a dress shirt and slacks. And while his shirt was a little tight, I didn't mind at all. Especially as it let me take in his lean — yet well defined — arms.

I felt my mouth begin to dry at the thought of how good this man might look with his shirt off.

"Is that Lou Howard?" Chase interrupted my train of thought, as he pointed off into the corner of the room. "Isn't he the team captain?"

I glanced over to where Chase pointed, and took in the spectacle that Lou was putting on. "Yep," I sighed, "that's him alright."

The VIP section of the club was more than simply an exclusive lounge. It had its own sequestered bar, and even an indoor swimming pool.

And beside that pool, with his half-naked body sprawled across one of the poolside loungers, lay our esteemed Dashing Colonels captain, Lou Howard.

Bent over Lou — licking what looked like salt off Lou's naked torso — was some platinum blond. And as soon as she licked the salt, she followed it up by downing a shot.

As the blond let loose a whoop of delight, I watched on bemused, as the small crowd around them whooped along with her. The crowd then began to chant, urging the blond on, as she grabbed Lou's head and drew him into a sloppy careless kiss.

"Are those two together?" Chase asked, curiosity coloring his voice as I watched him look on, transfixed by the scene.

If this was the first time you'd been to a Dashing Colonel's party, then the mayhem that happened at these shindigs would have you gawking.

But I was used to them now, and the craziness that happened when me and my teammates let loose after a game, didn't faze me.

In fact, Lou was only one of the reasons why these Dashing Colonel's parties were infamous around town. Every time we threw a bash, we would put on a show that could at best be called 'champagne-fueled anarchy'.

Our team manager made sure we always hired out the entire nightclub, so that he could try and reign in the team at the drop of a hat.

But glancing around the place — as all of my teammates lived it up with the other clubbers who'd managed to luck their way into an invite — it was obvious our manager's attempt to control our celebration had failed.

I took a quick swig from the small bottle of champagne in my hand, as I held back a chuckle. "No, Lou's not really a one-woman kind of guy. Besides," I paused a second to take a longer look at the platinum blond, "I don't recognize her, so she isn't one of the regular groupies."

Chase seemed to do a double take at that, dragging his attention away from the Lou-induced spectacle and turned towards me. "What about you?" He gestured at the room, sweeping a hand to indicate the thumping party. "Why aren't you out there with your friends?"

I sighed, reclining in my seat, grimacing as I shifted to relieve the dull pain in my left knee. I was drifting into old-man years — at least by footballing standards. And my body was starting to feel all of the combined years of tackles I'd taken throughout my career.

I glanced over at Lou, who despite being just three years my junior, was still bouncing around like a brash-new rookie. Lou was now apparently down on all fours, with the platinum blond now astride his back. She was throwing confetti at anyone they past by, as Lou carried her around the room.

I grinned at the scene, shaking my head as I chuckled aloud. Where Lou found the energy from, I did not know. Then again, his high-spirited character had also made Lou one of the youngest quarterbacks and football captains in the league. And I respected that.

I sensed Chase's attention begin to burn a hole into the side of my face, so I turned to him. And a touch of surprise took me when I noticed Chase's genuine interest in my answer.

I shrugged. "It's not for me," I admitted, handing over my champagne bottle, offering Chase a drink. He took it with a nod and took a swig as I continued. "I've done the whole *living it up* thing. But I guess I'm getting on in years now. I'm practically an old man."

Chase half-laughed half-choked on the swig of champagne. He leaned forward, and I slapped him on the back, helping him get through his brief coughing fit.

Once the coughing past, Chase gave me a meaningful look. "You are not an old man, at all."

Chase's eyes traced slowly down and then back up my body in appreciation. And I could feel the heat of a low-down tingle spread in my groin, as Chase took me in with hungry eyes.

When his gaze reached back up to meet mine, Chase seemed to catch himself staring, and tried to shake off the lustful look with a shake of his head.

Swallowing back a smirk, I caught a hint of blush touch Chase's cheeks as he stumbled over his words. "I meant that you look fit. I mean, that you look like you keep fit." Chase paused, bringing his fingers up to pinch the bridge of his nose in frustration. And this time I let loose the laugh I'd been holding back.

"I get you," I said, deciding to let him off from flustering any longer. "I know how good I look, I can't lie." I leaned back, puffing out my chest.

I wanted Chase to get a good look at what I was offering. And then maybe, later on tonight, I might be able to get a good look at what he had to *offer* too.

I knew I was picking up vibes off of Chase from the moment I'd met him, but I couldn't put my finger on it. I figured he would be another straight guy that I'd *'convert'* over to my side of the fence with a little bit of flirting. Plenty of men had been hardcore straight...that is until they'd met me.

But, it seemed like Chase was more bi-curious than I'd first figured. And that made things a lot more interesting.

Deciding to turn up my flirting game earlier than I'd planned, I leaned in, reaching to grasp the champagne bottle from his hands. I made sure to let my fingers linger on his for a long moment, before taking the cool glass container into my own.

"So, you often go around telling guys how fit they are? Or am I just that special?"

This time Chase's hint of blush turned much redder, as he floundered. "I didn't mean it like that, I only meant..."

I waved him off with a grin. "I'm playing with you, dude," I said as I leaned back into my seat. This time, I let my eyes wantonly rake themselves over Chase's body, wanting him — needing him — to see the heat behind my gaze. "I get it. There's nothing wrong in a little mutual appreciation."

I watched as Chase's mouth gaped open at that, genuine surprise on his face at my brazenness. It's rare that I'd be this publicly bold when flirting with another guy. Normally I'd feel things out a little — usually via a dating app — so that I could stay discreet.

Yet there was something about Chase that made me want to throw caution to the wind. I wanted him to want me. And from the tightening happening in my pants as Chase leaned in towards me — as though drawn by our combined magnetism — it looked like he wanted me too.

"Hey, I've got a lot more of this," I gestured with the bottle of champagne, "back at my place. We can go there now if you'd like, it'll be quieter. What do you say?"

A moment of confusion colored Chases face as I watched him struggle to register what I was asking — or rather, what I was *really* asking.

And then, as quickly as that confusion came, it went. Chase rubbed his chin thoughtfully as he pinned me with those beautiful green orbs.

"Make that a beer, and I'm game."

I smiled widely, not bothering to hide my genuine admiration. Seems like Chase was a man after my own heart.

"Alright then, let me go grab my..." I began as I moved to stand. But, before I could finish my sentence, an ear-splitting alarm suddenly went off.

Utterly confused, I turned to look at Chase, my own puzzlement reflected in his face. And then before either of us could utter another word, the fire sprinklers overhead went off and started to douse us — and everyone else in the room — with water.

Chapter 5

CHASE

One minute I was looking into Jake's eyes, trying to ignore the heat flooding my face as I did so. The next minute, the roof seemingly opened up, and we both were getting soaked with water.

It were as though the universe knew in that moment that I needed a cold shower. And, as luck would have it, the universe provided it in spades.

"What the hell is going on?"

"What is happening?"

Jake and I spoke over each other as we rushed from our seats, while pandemonium erupted in the club. Everyone around us shrieked and whooped in delight, hands raised high into the air as though the DJ had just dropped a beat.

"We should go," Jake said as his hand curled around my forearm. We both then laughed along with the other revelers, as we navigated our way through the crowd.

It didn't take us too long to make our way out through the side door fire escape. But, it was long enough to see us both completely drenched from head-to-toe.

Jakes hand dropped from my arm, but I continued to trail after him.

I tucked a hand into my soaking shirt collar, bringing the uncomfortably wet material away from my neck. I wasn't looking forward to making my way home in these sopping wet clothes.

As we wandered through the crowd, Jake grasped the shoulder of a passer-by. The stranger was big and broad, but still a touch shorter than Jake.

'This guy could hold his own on the football field with the Dashing Colonels,' I thought to myself.

And, as it turns out, I was right.

"Tony, hey!" Jake began, clearly familiar with the stranger, who immediately turned to face him. Tony grinned as he took in Jake.

"Lucky! Bro!" Tony said a little too loudly — looking a touch tipsy — as he grasped Jake's proffered hand. The two men then pounded together in a heartfelt shoulder-bump of a greeting. "This is all so crazy, right?"

"Yeah, yeah," Jake agreed smoothly. I watched him pat Tony on the shoulder, calming down his over-excited friend. "Do you know what happened back in there?" Jake jutted a thumb over his shoulder back at the club.

"Bro, it was Zeke," Tony replied, swaying a little on his feet. "All of us rookies dared him to pull the alarm cause Zeke kept saying that it wasn't hooked up to anything." Tony paused to half-hiccup/half-laugh at that. "Now there are fire engines out here and all that 'ish!" he continued, pointing over at the two red engines that had come to a stop outside the building.

"Damn," Jake said under his breath, before speaking aloud. "Coach is not gonna be happy about this. Fire engines at the party? Twice in one month?"

Tony appeared to sober up quickly at that. A look of mild dread crossed Tony's face so suddenly that it was almost comical. "Oh crap. You're right," Tony rubbed a hand across his features, before giving Jake a concerned look. "It wasn't me, Luck, seriously. Bro, it was Zeke. I was just standing there, I wasn't doing anything."

Jake nodded, patting Tony on the shoulder. "Don't worry, I got you."

Tony's seemed placated by that. And his worried features quickly transformed back into the lazy grin from earlier.

"Thanks bro!" Tony said as he ran off into the crowd with arms raised and a whoop. He then did a running jump onto the backs of a group of guys stood further down the street.

Jake shook his head, and gestured at the men who were all yelling it up with Tony. "The rookies." Jake said by way of explanation. It didn't explain much, but I nodded in agreement, as though I knew what he was on about.

"Come on, lets get clear of the building, and let the fire officers do their work."

I continued to trail after Jake, as we made our way across the street. And as soon as we came to stop on the other side of the road, Jake turned to grin at me. "Those sprinklers were no joke, for a moment there I thought they were going to drown us."

I nodded, half-distracted by the sight of Lou's platinum blond friend from earlier, wandering nearby. She was just as soaked through as myself and Jake. And long black mascara streaks lined her face, as she made her way past us.

I shook my head, running a hand through my wet hair to slick it back. "I'm certainly not looking forward to traveling back home looking like this," I said as a crowd of our fellow clubbers began to gather around us on the roadside.

I plucked helplessly at my shirt, the material barely leaving my skin, before sticking to me again.

"Oh I don't know," Jake paused for a moment, long enough to make me turn my gazed towards him in question. "You don't look half bad."

I recognized the lust in Jake's eyes as he took in my shirt appreciably. But, his own attire tore my attention away from his gaze, as I became transfixed by his taut muscle.

Jake had unbuttoned his shirt completely, as he tried to shake off the excess water clinging to the fabric.

Yet, it wasn't his shirt that held my attention. Instead it was the eight-pack abs, (and unspeakably buff chest), that I couldn't tear my gaze away from.

"Speak for yourself," I said with genuine awe at how incredibly built this guy was. I knew footballers had to workout and keep themselves in shape. But, Jake was ridiculously cut.

It took a tightening twinge from my dick to bring me back into the moment. Catching myself, I coughed to cover my staring, as I angled away from Jake.

The last thing I needed Jake to see was my growing erection against the wet skin-clinging fabric of my pants!

So instead, I made a show of searching the crowd, and began looking for Tyler.

"Well, um, I should see if I can find my friend..." I began, as I surreptitiously moved a hand across the front of my pants to hide my rising shame.

This hadn't been the first time my dick reacted to the sight of a well-muscled man. But, all of those previous times had been easier to hide — or at least deny.

I mean, who doesn't do a double take at the gym?

I felt Jake's large warm palm rest on my middle back. The heat of it felt good, and it was doing me no favors in getting my erection back under control.

"You should come back to my place," Jake said as he moved to stand next to me, jostling aside a couple who were stood nearby. He lowered his voice as he spoke to me, and me alone. "I've got some clothes that you can change into. Besides, you don't want to travel back home soaked like that. Trust me," Jake gave me an easy smile that I couldn't help but to return. "I've played long games in the pouring rain, and it is not fun."

I raised an eyebrow, letting a lazy grin spread across my face. "I'm sure your clothes aren't going to fit me." And I wasn't wrong. Jake was nearly twice my size — and from what I could see through his still open shirt, not an ounce of it was fat.

Besides earlier, when I felt that Jake was flirting with me, it all felt like a game. It was simply something fun to think about, but not to actually follow through on.

I wasn't actually seriously contemplating taking Jake up on his offer. I didn't even think Jake's earlier invite was even real.

Maybe Jake was the sort of straight guy who liked to flirt non-stop and didn't know when to turn it off — even around other straight men.

Yet, as soon as that thought arrived, I dismissed it. I knew I was lying to myself. Straight men don't flirt with straight men. And I should know, cause I'm as straight as they come.

'Aren't I?' I questioned myself.

I then realized I'd remained silent a little too long, as I noticed Jake's eyebrows hitch up in anticipation of my answer.

I rubbed the back of my neck before answering. "I'll need to call my friend to let him know where I'm at. He's probably somewhere in this crowd too," I said with a quick glance around me.

"Sure." Jake's sounded skeptical, as though he had caught me out in a lie. "Is that the Tyrese guy you mentioned before?"

I grinned, remembering my previous attempts at lying — badly I might add — to cover for my friend. "Yeah, but..."

Before I could finish my sentence, my cellphone started ringing, and the thrum of it's vibration startled me.

Snagging my phone from my back pocket, I breathed a silent sigh of relief, as I noticed that my phone had somehow managed to stay dry.

On the screen, I saw Tyler's name, and quickly answered.

"Hey, Chase!" Tyler greeted, sounding excitedly out of breath. "Where are you? Did you manage to get out of the club?"

"Yeah, I got out as soon as the water started coming down," I answered, whilst silently indicating to Jake that it was my friend on the phone. Moving a little aways from Jake, I placed one finger in my other ear, as I tried to hear Tyler through the noise of the surrounding crowd. "Where are you?"

"I'm outside too. And, boy, I was worried you'd gotten grabbed by the guards and they'd tossed you out. I was searching for you this whole time."

A pang of guilt snatched at me for a moment. I'd been hanging out with the football team that Tyler obsessed over. And I hadn't even thought to try and get Tyler into the VIP room with me. Before I could begin to tell him that and apologize, Tyler continued.

"...but then I met this hot chick. We started hitting it off. And Chase, I think I'm in here."

"Dude, what? For real?"

Tyler wasn't the most suave when it came to women. He was more of a numbers-game kind of guy.

I'd once seen him hit on 10 different girls in a row at a party, until the final one took pity on him, and gave him her number.

It was a fake number. But, he got an 'A' for effort.

"Seriously!" A sound of genuine shock colored Tyler's voice. "When I was looking for you, I saw her. And dude she is an Angel sent from above. She was hanging near the VIP area looking put out. But I figured, hey, gotta take my shot!"

For a moment I wondered if he might have met the girl Jake had been trying to escape from before. But I shrugged off the coincidence. "Good for you, dude. You get her number?"

"Better, she invited me back to her place tonight."

I grinned at the happiness in Tyler's voice. Hopefully he wasn't about to instantly fall in love with this woman he'd just met. Still, good for him.

"I know you're my ride back, but can you get a hotel room overnight? I gotta get laid, dude! You think you can find somewhere for one night?"

Tyler had done this sort of thing to me before. He'd persuade me to come out on a night out, and then ditch me if he got a lucky break with a girl.

And usually, I'd be annoyed at him for a short while, before realizing that he really didn't get that many lucky breaks. So, it was tough to stay mad at my friend for too long.

Besides, this time was different.

I angled around to face Jake. He was stood with a couple guys, sagely listening to them talk, as they gestured animatedly at the club. In fact, they looked like a couple of the guys from the group of rookies Jake had referred to earlier.

Jake must have felt me looking at him, because he tilted his head towards me, his eyes meeting my gaze with an unspoken question.

"Yeah, I think I can figure out a place to stay overnight," I told Tyler, letting a grin spread across my face as I gave Jake a short nod.

Chapter 6

JAKE

I had no idea why I was feeling nervous.

Chase wasn't the first guy I'd brought back to my place. Not by a long shot.

But when he entered my open-plan apartment, I wanted to impress him.

My luxury apartment alone was enough to impress anyone. I should know, I'd bought it for that reason alone.

I was a young brash kid with more money than I'd known what to do with at the time. So of course I spent it on cars, apartments and women — and discreetly on men too.

Yet, I didn't want a throwaway encounter with Chase. I wanted — *inexplicably* — something a little more.

Which was why all of my flirting game had gone right out of the window the moment he'd entered my home. And I didn't follow my usual get-laid routine of music, low lighting, and drinks — *before getting right into the hard bang.*

Instead, I had simply offered Chase a towel — and the use of the shower in the master bathroom — and left a change of clothes out for him on my bed.

And that left me sat on the couch like a damn fool, wondering where my confidence had gotten to.

'You're too inside your head,' I told myself, getting up to wander across the apartment to pour myself a whiskey. I stopped short from actually pouring a drink when I heard the sounds of the shower suddenly stop.

Re-stopping the whiskey bottle, I took that moment to decide that I wanted a clear head. I needed to get things back on track.

'Damn it,' I chastised myself as I wandered back to sit on the couch. It was then that the doors to my apartment bedroom opened.

"Jake, you're bathroom is nearly as big as my whole apartment." Chase said as he made his way into the room.

I turned around and was met by the sight of Chase wearing nothing other than my bath towel wrapped around his waist. Water still dripped from his hair, as he dried it with a hand towel.

And what a sight it was to behold.

Lickable defined abs, firm pecs, and the firm V-shape of a swimmers body. He wasn't bulky like the footballers I surreptitiously gawked at in the team locker room.

Instead, Chase was exactly my type, and looked firm enough to take my passionate pounding. And yet I knew I could still easily lift him up and down, as I'd make him bounce on my dick.

Damn it, I was becoming so horny thinking about it, but resisted adjusting my hardening member.

I cleared my throat before answering. "Thank you."

I bit back a groan. *Thank you? Seriously, that's the best you could come up with?'*

If Chase noticed my awkwardness, he spared my blushes by not pointing it out. "You're welcome," he said with a shrug, before casting a glance around the apartment. "So, where am I sleeping tonight?"

The cocky reply *'in my bed'* almost fell from my lips, before I caught myself. I didn't want the night to end yet, but I didn't want to rush things either.

God, this was all so much easier when I picked up men over a dating app.

We'd exchange a few faceless pictures of our chests, and that's all it would take. By the time the guys arrived at my apartment, there was no pretense, no second guessing.

Hell, there'd barely be any conversation, before I was leading them half-naked to go fuck in the sauna.

And that's when it hit me.

"I've got a sauna," I blurted out, then paused before further explaining. "It's where I go to relax after a game to help loosen up my muscles. And besides, the night is still young." I gave my wall clock a quick glance. The time read 2:12AM.

I tried not to look sheepish. "Well, the night is still young somewhere, right?" I stood up, and made my way over to Chase. "And before you say no, you have to try it. It really is a great way to unwind."

Chase rubbed his chin for a moment, then shrugged. "Sure, let's go."

The sauna did always help me to relax after a game, I was not lying about that.

But it turns out, it also helped me to release much of the anxiousness I'd been feeling earlier too.

I'd stripped down, albeit not in front of Chase — *at least not yet*. And now my own attire matched his.

Wearing nothing but a long fluffy white towel around my waist, I sat in the steam filled room. And, letting the humidity do it's work, I reclined back onto the bench.

On the bench opposite me, sat Chase. With his eyes closed, he looked like he was enjoying the hot atmosphere as much as I was.

Thankful that his eyes were closed, I ogled Chase openly, my gaze tracking the trails of sweat that beaded on his skin. My mouth felt dry as that sweat made it's way down — *way down* — to his navel.

I could feel my cock thicken with excitement, as I pondered what was hiding underneath that towel.

"You're right," Chase's voice startled me out of my fantasy, as I tore my gaze up from his crotch. And my eyes rose to find his eyes meeting my own.

There was no way Chase didn't see me ogling him. "Right about what?" I said, sitting up a little straighter.

"About this place," Chase answered, waving a hand around the sauna. The sauna was situated on the my large outdoor balcony. And a large glass window looked out over the city skyline. "It is relaxing."

"I knew you'd like it," I said confidently, as I glanced around. "It never fails to impress."

"So, you bring a lot of people in here?"

"What?" I asked, curiously.

"You said the sauna impresses, so I figured..." Chase let his voice trail off.

Was I hearing a touch of jealousy in his tone?

"Wouldn't you like to know?" I said with a cocky grin, enjoying the fact that Chase seemed put out that others had been here before him.

"Is that why you invited me here?"

"What do you mean?" I asked, as I pretended to be genuinely confused.

Chase sighed and ran a hand across his face. "Look, I don't know how guys do this with each other, or anything. But...," Chase paused with a helpless shrug of his shoulders, "...are you hitting on me? I mean, this entire night, you've been coming onto me."

Now was my chance.

I rose and moved across the room to sit down next to Chase. And I was pleased when I noticed that he didn't move away when I sat down close to him.

Reaching out, I gently placed a hand on Chase's knee as I pinned him with my eyes. "I was beginning to think you hadn't noticed," I said. My voice was low and taut with need, as I squeezed his knee.

On top of that, my towel was starting to tent with the physical manifestation of my urgent need. Still, I saw no point in trying to play it off now.

I hadn't been sure if Chase was at least bi-curious, or straight as an arrow.

My gaydar wasn't the greatest, but then, I'd never needed to hone it. When it came to my gay dating app flings, the question was never in doubt.

But now, looking deep into Chase's lust-filled eyes, I had no doubt in my mind that he wanted me almost as much as I wanted him.

Only question now was which one of us would make the first move.

"Fuck it," Chase whispered harshly. And too my surprise, he reached up and cupped the back of my head, drawing us into a kiss.

Chapter 7

CHASE

The anticipation had been killing me.

I'd been waiting all night for Jake to make a move, curious about how it would feel to be hit on by a good looking guy. I half-expected him to try something in the car-ride over here. And I definitely thought he would at least offer to join me in the shower.

*Or **something** — anything at all.*

In fact, we'd been sat in the sauna in near silence for ten minutes, before I finally broke the tension.

I'd never done this before in my life — kiss a guy, I mean. And I certainly didn't think I would be discovering my sexuality by kissing a pro-fucking-footballer!

Yet here I was, tonguing a man whose half-naked body could grace the front page of any bodybuilding magazine in the world.

As our kiss deepened, I felt Jake move his hand from my knee to curl it around my waist. Jake's body clearly dwarfed mine in shear magnitude, yet I didn't feel intimidated as he tugged me in close.

Jake let loose a low grunt as his tongue pushed past my lips, penetrating and demanding access to my mouth.

And I let him — *God help me, I let him* — stroke his strong fingers across the sweat soaked skin of my hip, coming dangerously close to my groin.

After long moments, we both eventually pulled back a little from our kiss, as I tried to catch my breath.

'Fuck,' I thought.

"Fuck," I repeated, but this time out loud as I took in Jake's cocky grin.

"I know, right?" Jake said, his mouth just a whisper away from mine. "And that's only a taste of how I'm gonna make you feel."

My dick was hard as rock now, the soft fabric of my towel doing nothing to hide it. But, with a quick glance down into Jake's lap, I could see that he was just as firm and as ready as I was.

'But am I ready to go further?'

The doubt-filled question clouded my thoughts for a moment, right up until I felt Jake shift his hand from my hip towards my groin. I hissed with pleasure when his hand brushed over the front of my towel, his fingertips slowly curling around my thickened shaft.

I let loose a long slow moan, my eyes closing as I enjoyed the feel of his hand grasping my manhood through the fabric. Jake held my cock loosely, while I struggled to fight the almost primal need to thrust up into his palm.

"Do you want more?" Jake whispered the words into my ear as his loose grip began to manipulate my hard-on. "I want to taste you," Jake breathed, hot and heavy before shifting his lips to peck a kiss onto my neck. "I want your dick in my mouth," Jake continued, slipping his hand from my cock, to rest on my thigh. "Tell me you need me to suck your dick."

I opened my eyes to find Jake looking at me, his eyes searching my features as he waited on my answer.

"I need you to suck my dick," I said, my vocal chords tight with need.

I stayed seated on the bench as, (without another word), Jake slipped from his seat and slid onto the floor in front of me.

I watched as he grasped my towel, which was tenuously still wrapped around my waist, and pulled at it to reveal my cock.

Relaxing my hips, I spread my legs apart, giving Jake room to nestle himself in between them, as he quickly got to work on my bulbous glistening cock-head.

Slipping it between his lips, Jake sucked my cock down whole with a spine-tingling swallow. I groaned out loud leaning back against my seat, as Jake's mouth slid up and down my dick, his rough tongue running along the underside of my manhood.

My balls jumped with excitement when Jake began to flick his tongue off the very tip of my cock with each rise of his bobbing head. The intensity of it was almost too much, as I thrust my hips towards his face.

It didn't take too long for that familiar feeling of incredibly intense pleasure begin to reach it's peak. And all I could focus on was the twinned sounds of Jake's mouth slurping my hard shaft — and my repeated grunt after grunt as I pounded into his face.

We filled the steamy sauna room with a chorus of carnal delight, as I reach forward to place a hand on the back of Jake's head. "Fuck yes," I said through gritted teeth, "yes, like that. Suck it deep, so deep down your throat."

I was thrusting so hard now, holding Jake's head in place, as I felt my cock-head brush the back of his throat. How he'd kept himself from gagging, I had no idea. But in that moment, I was just grateful he was taking my dick as deep as it would go. And my balls tapped repeatedly against Jake's chin as I humped his wet mouth.

"I'm gonna come," I whispered, my ball-sack tightening, readying to release itself. I was on the fleeting edge, and I wanted to explode!

"I'm coming, damn fuck! Fuck! FUCK!" I cried out loud when my body became rigid with every spurting string of hot cum ejaculating from my dick.

Chapter 8

JAKE

Chase held my face so tightly against his body that I could barely breathe, as he blew his hot salty release down my throat.

But, a few moments later, his body finally relaxed, and his death grip on the back of my neck soon loosened.

"Oh shit!" Chase said, breathless, the words haltingly spoken as he gasped for breath. "That was incredible!" Chase then paused for a moment, before continuing. "Damn. I didn't mean to make you...," he moved to rest a hand on my cheek. "Did you swallow my, well, you know..." Chase asked, looking shamefaced.

I leaned forward, and planted a kiss on Chases lips, moving my hands to rest them on either side of his hips. In one move, I tugged him forward towards me, till there was almost no space left to separate us. And the only room left was reserved for my erect hard cock nestled between our bodies.

Sometime during my blowing Chase's dick, my towel had become untucked, and I was now knelt fully naked in front of him.

I leaned in. "You didn't make me. I wanted to." And then I kissed him, pushing my tongue into his mouth, so that Chase could taste his cum on my tongue.

We stayed like that for a long minute, our tongues warring with each other, as we kissed. And all the while, my hard cock trembled with anticipation.

I needed some relief. And my body rippled with a lust so electrified that Chase had to have felt it too.

Chase pulled his lips away from mine, a satiated gaze in his green orbs, as he began to reach for my dick. "I've never sucked a dick before, but I'm gonna make you come so hard that…"

Chase halted his actions when I placed a gentle palm on his forearm.

I didn't want him to suck my dick. I wanted more.

I needed to take Chase so much deeper than simply his mouth could allow.

"Not like this," I said, as Chase gave me a curious look at the quick shake of my head. "Let's go to my bedroom," I explained as I rose to my feet and held out a hand to him.

Chase sat on the corner of my bed giving me an almost comically skeptical look. "You wanna fuck me in the ass?"

I tossed the small bottle of lube I held onto the bed beside him, and then moved to kneel in front of Chase. He spread his legs, letting me nestle up close to him, as I once again placed my hands on his hips.

Being this close to his naked body was almost intoxicating, as sweat still beaded on his chest. My erection hadn't gone anywhere either, (in the short walk from the sauna to my bedroom), but now I was almost painfully hard.

I planted a quick kiss on his lips, before relaxing back on my heels. "You are gonna love it," I began, letting my hand trail up along his taut torso, rising up to his nipple. I flicked the tip of it as I continued. "And I'll go nice and slow."

Chase ran a hand through his hair as he cast me a dubious look. "I don't know. I've had like maybe a single finger up in my ass, once. Only once." Chase gave my cock a meaningful look. "I'm not even sure I could fit your whole dick up there."

"OK, I get it, it's cool…" I said, trying not to sound put-out, but I did not want to push him into anything. Yet, before I could say another word, Chase interrupted.

"No wait," he rushed out, reaching out to place a hand on my chest. "I'm not saying no, I'm simply trying to say that I've never done this before."

I tilted my head a little and smiled. Chase's blush returned, creeping across his cheeks. "You don't have to do this, you know. It really is cool if you don't want to."

Chase quickly shook his head. "Nah, I wanna try this. First time for everything, right?" he said with a chuckle.

I kissed him again, letting my lips linger on his for a hot moment. "Shuffle back on the bed a bit," I whispered, but Chase heard every word, and eagerly inched back onto the mattress.

I reached over to grasp the bottle of lube. "Flip over onto your front, I need to get you ready." Without a single word of question — and looking almost as excited as I felt — Chase did as he was told.

Turning over, he lay on his front, his naked firm ass prone and ready for me.

'Not ready, not quite yet.' I thought to myself.

Quickly opening the bottle of lube, I liberally coated my fingers with the stuff. Planting one hand on Chase's butt cheek, I eased it aside to find his tight entrance.

I covered Chase's hole with lube, covering every inch with the slippery stuff before I began.

"I'm going to go in with only one finger, so relax and breathe."

"Umm hmm," came Chase's muffled reply, his mouth buried in the silk fabric sheets of my bed.

Slowly, I eased in a single finger into his hole, and to my surprise, it slipped in easier than I'd thought. It was nice and tight, but Chase had clearly kept his muscles relaxed enough to take in the penetration.

"That feel good?" I asked Chase as I tore my attention away from his ass to find Chase looking at me awkwardly over his shoulder.

"Yeah, that kinda does," Chase said.

I nodded, then returned back to focusing on his tight hole. I slid my finger out, and then pushed back in again, but this time with two fingers.

Now I heard Chase let loose a grunt, so I paused half-way in, only knuckle-deep. "You want me to keep going?"

Chase lifted his head, and uttered a breathless, "God yes!"

Chuckling, I continued to push my fingers into him right up to the hilt. Except, this time, instead of pausing there, I nimbly felt around for his sensitive spot.

Brushing it lightly, I grinned when Chase gave out a long slow groan. I'd found his Guy-spot.

Chase lifted his head up, "don't stop doing that," he told me, and I continued to lightly rub there for a few more seconds, before pulling my fingers back out.

"Aww, man," Chase said, turning over to look at me over his shoulder. He was gripping the sheets of the bed now, but he had a put-out look on his face. "That really felt good, I wanted you to keep going."

I laughed as I rose to my feet and began to pour lube all over my cock. "Oh, don't you worry," I said, giving my dick a couple of quick lube-slicked pumps of my fist. "I'm going to keep going for sure."

Moving forward, with one hand I propped myself up over Chase's body. With my other hand, I pointed my cock-head right at his sweet back entrance.

My cock was way bigger than my two fingers, but Chase's eagerness let me know that he was ready to take every inch of my manhood.

So slowly, *oh so slowly*, I slipped every single inch right up his ass until I was balls deep. And with every single slippery inch, Chase groaned with delight.

"You like that, huh?" I said, as I slipped back out, and then thrust back in again. God, he felt so good around my cock. "You really like that?" I pulled back and thrust back into him again.

"Yes, um-mm," Chase's words were muffled by the blankets he was biting down on as I pressed my manhood into him again and again.

His ass felt as tight as I'd been imagining all night. And soon my slow steady thrusts became urgent pounds, as I humped his firm buttocks with everything I had.

With each push I grunted, delighting in the feel of Chases inner walls rubbing against my cock. And with each pullout, Chase moaned, as my cock-head rubbed his sensitive walls.

Leaning forward, I lay my body flush against Chase's back, needing to feel more of him against me. I hooked my arms under Chase's arms, leveraging myself into a position that would let me take him even deeper.

Chase's legs widened, his thighs splayed out as he wordlessly invited me to take him harder. And I took him, pounding as our sweat-drenched bodies came together over and over again.

Our chorus of grunts and moans gradually became louder and louder. And I was pretty sure my neighbors could hear us now.

"Chase, ugh, Chase, yes. So good..." I planted kisses on the back of Chase's neck between each word. "Yes, God, I need this. God I need to come in your ass. Fuck!" I gasped, feeling my balls grow tight, and my body become taut, as I teetered on the edge of release. "I'm Almost There!"

But, it was Chase's voice that did it for me. "Shit...Oh Shit! I'm Coming AGAIN!" Chase yelled out, right as my orgasm hit me hard.

It was all too much. So with one final thrust, I yelled out, as my body became rocked by the force of my release.

Chapter 9

CHASE

My second orgasm of the night hit me so hard, my toes curled as the heat of it flooded my body from head to toe.

Between the friction of the sheets against my cock, and the repeated press of Jake's muscled body pressing down on me, I'd all but been humping the bed.

But more than that, it was the intoxicating feel of Jakes dick rubbing my prostate again and again, that eventually wrung another release out of me.

I didn't even know I could do that!

"Fuuuuuuuuccck!" I drew out the swear, my voice lowering and becoming tight, as Jake pressed into me deep with one final urgent push, before collapsing.

I felt his breath hot and heavy on the back of my neck, the heated fire of his body now flush on top of me. It felt good, listening to Jake gasp for breath.

'I'd done that to him,' I thought, unable to stop myself from grinning at the fact that I had a pro-footballer whispering sweet nothings into my ear.

"That was amazing," Jake told me, planting a quick peck on my neck, before lifting himself up. I felt pleasurable relief as he slid his cock all the way out of my ass, and then dropped down on the bed to lie beside me.

I turned on my side, feeling different somehow — the ache in my butt-hole obviously — but also something more.

"I told you that you'd love it." Jake's eyes turned down, his gaze pointedly fixed upon the sopping wet-spot I'd left on his bed.

I dipped a finger into the sticky pool of my own cum. "Yeah, well. At least the wet spots over the duvet, right? Neither one of us needs to sleep on it."

With a chuckle, Jake reach out to gently grasp my sticky-fingered hand. "Oh, I don't think either one of us is going to do any sleeping quite yet." And with that, he pulled my fingers into his mouth and licked them clean.

Jake and I didn't fall asleep until well into the morning. There was still so much more of our bodies we wanted to explore. And it was late-afternoon, when I awoke groggily to the sound of my phones message notification bell sound going off.

Jake lay on the bed beside me, sprawled out and fast asleep, the covers barely hiding his lower half. I took in the display, taking in every muscled sinew that I could lay my eyes on.

I became so distracted by watching Jake sleep, that it took a second notification bell to bring my attention back to my phone.

Grasping my phone from the bedside table, I read the message.

TYLER: Where r u C? I banged the chck!

I grinned at my phone, glad that both Tyler and I had managed to get our rocks off this weekend.

"Everything alright?" Jake's voice sounded deeper than usual, the husk of it thickened by sleep.

Placing my phone back down on the table, I shuffled around to lay on my back, leaving the bedsheets to messily pool at my waist. "Yeah, it's good. My friend was simply checking in."

Jake turned onto his side, his head propped up in one hand, as he gave me a questioning look.

"So, you and your friend...Ty, something? You two good friends? Or are you..."

Seeing where his thought process was going, I mentally scoffed at the idea. "His name's Tyler and he's my best friend. But, he's only a friend. And he's straight as an arrow."

Jake hummed in acknowledgment before replying. "Yeah, but so were you, yesterday."

I did a double take. Jake wasn't wrong. *'But then again...'*

"I think I've always wondered what it would be like to be with a guy," I answered honestly. "But I grew up in a small town. So, there was **no** chance I was ever going to explore the idea. Or take a chance on hitting on some local."

The silence that followed my admission was uncomfortably long. Still, I found a look of understanding on Jakes features, not one of derision.

"I get it. A little too well actually," Jake shrugged helplessly. "I've played football my whole life. And while I've always been bisexual, I've had to keep one side of my sexuality hidden away."

"That must have been tough," I prompted, wanting to hear more about Jake's past. But he simply shook his head, as though trying to shake off the vulnerability of the conversation.

"What I'm trying to say is," Jake sighed, before continuing. "I want to explore this," he waved a hand between us, "and see where this goes. I really think we have something here. But..."

Jake let his words trail off, and I quickly filled in the blank. "You want to keep it on the down-low."

Jake nodded. "At least for now. That way there's no pressure on us."

"OK. I'm fine with that for sure," I agreed, more than happy to keep things between ourselves.

I wasn't sure what last night meant for me in the big scheme of things — *was I gay now, or maybe bi?* However, what I was certain about, was that the last thing I wanted was to try and figure it all out in the public eye.

"And what about Tyler?" Jake asked, a hint of jealously coloring his voice.

I scoffed out loud this time. "Seriously, Jake. You are getting jealous over a guy that I see as my brother. Really, he and I are just friends." I turned on my side and mirrored Jake's stance, propping my head in my hand.

"And don't you think it's a little too early in this relationship to be playing the exclusivity card? You wanna exchange promise rings or something?" I said with a grin.

Jake growled playfully, reaching forward to grab my waist. In one strong move, he dragged me towards him, tucking me in close to his body. Jake let his lips hover over mine as he spoke. "I promise that I don't want to share you with anyone."

And with that, Jake sealed that promise with a kiss.

THE END

Thank you so much for reading Hard Luck!

The next book in the 'First Time for Everything' series is available for purchase right now by visiting here: https://books2read.com/u/38WrPw

Or you can simply keep reading for a quick sneak peek into 'Hard Wright'...

HARD Wright

A Straight To Gay Romance Law Enforcement
Story
(First Time for Everything Series)
By B.T. Haiyes

Chapter 1

JOSH

"You ready to give up?" I stared down my opponent with a satisfied smirk.

My arm was bulging, the strength of my forearm pushed to the limit, as I held my opponents hand in place.

All around us the patrons in the bar let loose yells of encouragement — with my friends behind me loudest of them all.

I breathed slowly, keeping my cool even as the tabletop bit into my elbow, but I was determined to win this arm wrestling match.

My friends and co-workers from the police station were all cheering me on. I even heard someone behind me yell that I had to win this, or they'd never let me live it down.

I chuckled. I was confident I was going to win. So, I comfortably stared down the bulging-eyed red-faced man opposite, and held his hand firmly in place.

He, on the other hand, tried to put everything he had behind his.

When this guy tossed an open challenge of an arm wrestle our way — after he'd made a stupid remark about all police cops being unfit — I was the only one in my group who took him up on it.

This total stranger had wandered right up to me and my friends. We were all gathered in our favorite bar, raising one last glass in cheers to celebrate the fact that one of our own was retiring today.

Arthur, (my former training officer and a good friend of mine), was finally hanging up his hat. He'd lasted longer than most, calling it quits at the age of sixty.

So, when this kid — who looked barely a day over 21 — had come up to us with a chip on his shoulder, I figured I'd take him down a peg.

No way was I going to let some punk ruin my friends retirement party.

The kid — *Tate, I think his name was?* — had done a double take when he took in my well built six foot four inch frame.

Tate was no slouch either, I'd give him that. He had the frame — along with the douche-level sleeveless teeshirt to match — of a bodybuilder.

But, one thing about all of those muscles on him, was that while they may be pretty, they weren't as functional as the real strength I'd built up over the years.

Tate's face was now beet-red, and I laughed when he refused to give up. I had to hand it to him, he was tenacious.

I felt Arthur place a hand on my shoulder, and I glanced up. "Come on, Josh. Stop playing around with the kid," Arthur said with an amused look on his face. Waving a dismissive hand at my red-faced opponent, Arthur continued. "Just take the damn win."

I nodded. Turning my attention back towards Tate, I flexed my forearm, and in one fell swoop, slapped his hand down on the table.

The entire bar erupted into cheers and applause, and I was immediately swamped with pats on the back and 'atta boys' from my friends.

"You tried your best, kid," I said honestly, as the kid rose from his seat with a surly grumble. "But I was better. Not bad for a *pudgy* cop, I reckon."

Tate grunted noncommittally, and moved to rejoin his group of snickering friends. But, before he made it half a step, I spoke up. "I think you're forgetting something?"

The kid looked at me confused, until he saw me rubbing my fingers and thumb together in that universal 'money' motion. "Fifty bucks to the winner. That was our bet."

He let loose a low swear, and snatched his wallet from his back pocket.

Pulling a crisp fifty from it, the kid slapped it on the table, and then quickly hustled off through the jostling crowd to go lick his wounds with his friends.

Plucking the fifty off the table, I lifted it triumphantly into the air. "Daisy!" I yelled out, addressing the bartender.

Everyone at the station came here so often that we were on a first name basis with Daisy.

"The next round of drinks..." I clapped Arthur on the shoulder, as he raised his beer glass to me in congratulations, "...are On ME!" I shouted.

The bar erupted with noise once again, and over the sounds of celebration, Daisy shouted back. "I don't think that's gonna cover it," she said with a laugh, indicating the fifty in my hand. "But I'll put it on your tab."

I returned her smile, giving her a grateful wink, before turning to speak to Arthur. "And what will you be having, old man?" I gave his beer glass a short nod, "another beer, or maybe something a bit stronger?"

Arthur shook his head ruefully. "Enough with the *old man*. I can still plenty put you on your ass," he said with a chuckle. "Just another beer for me. My wife, Sandra, made me quit hard liquor. Hell, even my son has me trying out some of his craft beers." Arthur mirrored my look of disgust at the thought of those artisan drinks.

"Why would your son do that to you?" I said in mock horror, giving Arthur a comical look of concern, as I placed a hand on his shoulder. "Do you need another drink to wash away the memory?"

Arthur brushed off my hand with a chortle. "My boy's a good kid. But his taste in beer? He gets that from his mother."

"Well, that's why you'll never see me settling down," I said with a laugh.

Arthur paused for a moment at that, giving me a quickly sobering look.

'Ah shit,' I thought to myself. *'I recognize that look...'*

"Before you say it..." I began, but Arthur waved me off.

"I know you don't want to hear it Josh, but I gotta say it again. Look at this," Arthur waved a hand up at the banner that stretched out over the bar.

The banner read, *Happy Retirement — 25 Years Of Service.*

"Twenty five years. That's a hell of a long time on the force," Arthur continued, giving me a meaningful glance. "I've seen a lot over the years. A lot of bad stuff. But I stayed, and kept going for so long because I had something besides the job to live for."

It was an old argument that the two of us had over the years.

I joined the force at the age of 24. And Arthur — my former training officer — had taken me under his wing.

I'll be the first to admit that being a detective is pretty much my whole life. I've never wanted to do or be anything else.

Which also meant I had no time for dating. And at the age of 32, I still didn't feel ready yet to settle down with anyone. And I certainly didn't want the distraction of being in a committed relationship.

And, as a gay man, I wasn't attracting the kind of guy I wanted to settle down with. There are plenty of gay badge bunnies out there, but they were always more turned on by the idea of my job, than by me.

Don't get me wrong, one time hookups came a plenty — and I loved it. I'd simply hop onto a dating app, find a guy, and then get that release by the end of the night.

And then the next day I was right back at work. It worked for me — uncomplicated with no strings attached — and that's how I liked it.

"I hear ya, Arthur, I do." I draped a friendly arm around my friends shoulders. "But you don't have to worry about me. Tonight, all you need to worry about is getting another drink!"

As I began to lead Arthur over to the bar, one of our group suddenly yelled out. *"Arthur! Your son, Ben, is here!"*

And at that, both Arthur and I turned towards the entrance of the bar to find a blond-haired man entering the establishment.

"Ben!" Arthur called out to the man, hands raised, as he went over to greet him.

I watched on as the two men embraced for a long moment, before Arthur turned around to face the crowd. "My son Ben, everyone!" The crowd cheered in response.

It took a few more moments for the raucous celebration to come down a few notches, and I took that time to go and grab myself another beer.

While I watched Daisy pour my drink, I soon felt a tap on my shoulder.

Looking over, I saw Arthur standing side by side with Ben, with his arm draped around him.

And up close — now that I could see him much more clearly — Ben made me do a double take.

I hadn't gotten a good look at him from across the bar. But, getting up close to Ben now, this grown man looked nothing like he had done in Arthur's family photos.

In the photos — atop Arthur's desk back at the station — there had been a skinny college kid stood in between Arthur and his wife.

I'd never met Ben before. He was already a year into pre-med when I'd met Arthur, back when I was a rookie.

Still, I had heard plenty about the guy in passing. Arthur was incredibly proud of Ben.

So I did a poor job at hiding the look of surprise on my face, when Arthur introduced me to his pride and joy.

Ben stood only a few inches shorter than myself. Yet every inch of him seemed firm and surprisingly muscled for his slender yet well-built frame.

And Ben's tight white teeshirt and skinny jeans, didn't do much to hide his physique either. He still had that slender build from those pictures. However, now, taut sinewy muscle lined his biceps and forearms.

It seemed like Ben had filled out a lot over the last few years.

Between his dress sense, handsome features — and his crystal blue eyes — Ben looked next to nothing like Arthur. Except they both shared a very distinctive sharp square jaw.

"Josh? You alright?" Arthur asked, and I snapped my gaping mouth shut once I realized I'd been staring.

Arthur knew I was gay. In fact, the whole damn station knew I was gay. But, the last thing Arthur needed to know was that I found Ben attractive.

My good friend didn't have a problem with my sexuality, but he might have a problem with me personally if I made a move on Ben.

"Uh, yes, of course. I'm Josh," I quickly wiped my sweaty palm on my jeans, and held it out to Ben.

"Ben," the blond replied, as he clasped my hand firmly.

"Good to meet you," I continued, giving his hand a brief shake. Ben's grip was impressively firm. "Your dad's told me a lot about you."

"All of it good, I hope?" Ben said, his melodious voice captivating me.

"Mostly." I replied, chuckling at the shared affronted look on both Arthur's and Ben's faces. "He told me you are trying to get him to start drinking those terrible soda's that you call craft beer."

"Hey!," Arthur began, giving me a soft playful punch in the stomach. "But Josh is not wrong, Ben. They are bad."

"Come on dad, they were a hit back in college," Ben said with a smile. "Everyone wanted to try my line of craft beers."

"So it had the approval of college kids," I said with a chuckle and a shake of my head. "No wonder they liked it. They've never tried real beer..." Daisy tapped me on the shoulder, indicating the full beer glass she'd set on the bar beside me.

I plucked the glass up from the bar and offered it to Ben. "...a real beer such as this one."

Ben gave Arthur a glance, and then turned back to me.

"I'm the designated driver. That's why I'm here, to drive my dad home after the parties over."

Arthur scoffed. "One beer won't hurt. And if it turns into two or more," he continued with a shrug, "we can simply call a cab."

Ben thought about it for a moment, before going 'oh well' and grabbed the proffered beer.

"Arthur, come on over here! I want you to meet Burt!"

Someone in our group yelled over the din, and waved Arthur over to them.

"I'll be right back," Arthur said, giving Ben a pat on the back, before striding off towards the still waving man.

"Guess the old man is still as popular as ever," Ben said with a grin as he shuffled over to stand at the bar beside me.

"Yep, he's one of the good ones. Sad to see him go." I said with a rueful nod.

Ben paused to take a sip of beer. He gave it an approving nod. "That's pretty good," he said, before turning his next words to me. "And how do you and my dad know each other?"

"He used to be my training officer years ago. Arthur taught me everything I know."

Ben nodded, silent for a long moment, as though contemplating something. "And does my dad know about...?" Ben raised his eyebrows, giving me a meaningful glance that I couldn't interpret.

"Know about?" I didn't bother to mask the confusion in my voice.

"Does he know that you're..." Ben glanced around as though we were about to be heard over the surrounding din. "...gay?"

My mind did a double take, surprised by the question. I was not sure where this was coming from — or how he'd even guessed my sexuality — so I answered evenly. "Yes, he does. Is that a problem for you?"

Ben paused a moment, a touch of confusion in his eyes, before he began stumbling over his words. "No! No, I don't have a problem with it at all. Sorry, I've just realized how that sounded." Ben sheepishly rubbed the back of his neck. "Look, I was going to mention it before, but I didn't know if my dad knew."

I sighed. I did not know where this conversation was going. But, I'd dealt with enough phobic assholes in my life to know there is no talking them round. And the last thing I wanted to do was to get into a fight with Ben at Arthur's retirement party.

I straightened up, and made to move away. "I need to go and check on..."

Ben raised his hands in a sign of apology. "Wait! I'm not judging! God, I'm doing this all wrong. Let me start again." Ben took a long breath, and then dropped his hands and tucked them into his pockets. "I'm *B-Love24*."

I blanked out for a few seconds, before clocking on.

This was the guy I'd messaged a couple times yesterday via the KissFerno dating app. That popular dating app was my mainstay method for finding hookups.

Except, on KissFerno, Ben's profile had simply been a shirtless torso with his face cropped out. I, on the other hand, didn't feel the need to hide away my features. I was more than happy to put my face on the line...so to speak.

At my lingering silence, Ben gave me a small unsure smile. "Very nice to meet you, *J-Heart3000*."

I searched my memory, trying to think of a time when Arthur had ever mentioned his son was gay. But I was coming up blank.

"OK, well, I did not know that." This was awkward. There was a reason why I used KissFerno to meet men — and didn't bother going to Gay bars. Using technology let me keep my distance. And, with the bar scene, it is much too easy to stumble across a former fling. "Arthur never told me. But, good for you." I said with a curt nod.

"Yeah, well, I just wanted to say. Actually, I'm not sure why I mentioned it," Ben rubbed the back of his neck sheepishly. "I'm not even gay."

At that new piece of information, all I could muster up was a single stony-faced raised eyebrow.

Chapter 2

BEN

'Ah, shit,' I chastised myself. *'What the heck am I doing?!'*

From the moment I set eyes on Josh, I immediately recognized him from his KissFerno profile. And I'd done a double-take when I saw him standing beside my father.

When my dad led me over to the guy, I was sure Josh would recognize me from the app.

It was a silly concern though. I had kept my face cropped out of the half-naked photo of my profile picture.

And I'd only gone onto KissFerno out of boredom, looking for a little fun. Although, admittedly, I was a little drunk at the time — at least a few beers in.

I meant to tick the box indicating that I was *'Straight'*, but I must have mis-clicked the box titled *'Gay'*. And I hadn't even noticed my mistake until an hour after my profile went live.

The first couple of men who sent me a 'Kiss' — to indicate their interest in me — should have been my first clue. And, at first, I put it down to them having misread my profile.

But, it wasn't until the fifteenth Kiss, that it occurred to me to go and double check my profile.

Opening up the app, I logged in, and there it was. Right beside my naked-chested picture — in bold caps — the word 'GAY MALE' came up as my sexual orientation.

It probably didn't help matters either, that my description read that I was *'up for anything'* and *'looking for someone nearby'*.

Now, I know I should have simply taken down the profile immediately. I should have deleted it — be glad my face wasn't on it — and called it a day.

But, then I received a Kiss from Josh. And what I saw of him turned my head. Even as a straight guy, I gotta admit, Josh was incredibly good-looking.

Between his firm muscled torso and big forearms, Josh stood out from all the other guys that had reached out to me.

Yet, it was the dimpled smile Josh wore in his profile picture, that captivated my attention.

That smile alone was what led me to inexplicably send Josh a Kiss back.

Unfortunately, standing in front of Josh in the real world, there was no trace of that dimpled smile looking down at me now.

Instead, all I saw was a tense frown punctuated by a cool gaze.

"And you go on dating apps to? What exactly?" Josh's voice was even. But, I could still hear the tense touch of annoyance in his tone. "You like to catfish and play games?"

"No, it's not like that." I tried not to rear back a little. There was a real intensity to Josh. And his huge muscled body added a powerful sense of presence that dwarfed my own.

I'd put my foot in it again.

It happened all the time whenever I got nervous around someone. Which led to me being terrible at picking up women.

Yet, as it turns out — even on the other end of the Kinsey scale — I'm still incredibly bad at turning on the charm.

But, damn it, I wanted to say the right thing to Josh. "It's a funny story actually." I paused with a chuckle.

Josh said nothing.

Awkwardly, I bumbled on, trying to break the tension. "I mean, it's kinda funny...at least once you hear it."

That was certainly not the right thing to say.

Josh waved me off. "No need to explain," he said, stony-faced. I wanted to see his dimpled smile, but had no idea how to do that.

I opened my mouth to say something, but then I heard my dad yell out. "Ben! Ben! Come on over here. I want you to meet these guys!"

I gave Josh a small apologetic smile — one which he did not reciprocate — and turned around to wave over at my dad. "I'll be right there!" I called out, before spinning back toward Josh.

Yet I was met with nothing but air. Josh had slipped away in the mere seconds it had taken for me to wave. And with a quick glance around the room, I found him already laughing it up with a group of men a little further down the bar.

Slumping my shoulders with a sigh, I turned back around and made my way over towards my dad.

Chapter 3

JOSH

I t was well past midnight when the party finally began to wind down.

It had been a hoot — as friends both new and old — had dropped in at various times during the night to wish Arthur well.

I'd personally down a heck of a lot of beer, but still didn't feel tipsy. Instead, I simply felt a bit of a buzz. Yet, it was enough to let me know that I was not going to be driving home tonight.

So, I ordered a cab instead. And standing just outside the bar entrance archway, I took in the deep crisp air of the night.

While I waited, my fellow party stragglers wandered out of the bar. And as each one of them past me, I nodded my final good nights to them, as they made their way home.

I was all smiles, until I saw Ben wander out through the doors of the bar.

I gave him a stiff, but polite, nod of my head. "Goodnight then."

Ben moved to stand a little aways from me, but didn't move much further. Instead, to my slight annoyance, he leaned back against the brick wall on the other side of the archway.

Tucking his hands into his pockets, Ben made a show of shivering. "Doesn't feel all that good."

I grunted with a noncommittal sound as I turned away to look down the road.

"I mean, it's warmer in my college state. Not that much warmer, but it's different, you know?"

"Mm." My reply was as terse as I felt.

"I'm waiting for a cab to come and pick up dad and me." With my head turned away from him, Ben did not see my eyes roll back as he continued with this strained one-sided conversation. "I was only going to have one drink. But every one of dad's friends kept offering me a beer, so..."

"Um hmm." My jaw tensed with annoyance.

"Anyway, I've had a few too many. But it was still a great shindig. So, you waiting for a cab too?"

"Yup." I didn't bother to expand on my single word answer. Instead, I peered down at the toe of my boot, taking a moment to rub it to a shine against the back of my pants leg.

"That's great!" Ben's voice brightened at the news.

Curious, I relented, and finally peered over at Ben. And the earnestness in his eyes would've been endearing, if I wasn't still pissed off about our earlier encounter.

After our conversation, I'd made a point of carefully avoiding Ben for the rest of the night. And — I'm not ashamed to admit that — I was worried he'd whip out his phone, and pull up my profile. Only to then show it off to Arthur and everyone else.

"...we should all share a cab." Ben's enthusiasm didn't wane in the face of the return of my stony silence. "It'll be better than waiting all night for your cab to arrive."

"I live on the other side of town from Arthur. Eastside." I answered, feeling my iciness begin to melt a touch in the face of Ben's genuinely warm personality.

"Oh," Ben's shoulders dipped a little, making him appear very much like a sad puppy. I bit back the touch of a grin that threatened to reach my lips. "Guess sharing the cab doesn't make sense. But, the Eastside is rough. You like it there?"

I shrugged. "Was born and raised there my whole life. It can get rough at times, but that's why I stay near. That way I can help out my friends and neighbors at a drop of a hat."

Ben nodded at my answer with a broad smile. "You really are a man with a heart of gold, huh."

I scoffed. "Staying where you grew up is hardly worthy of a medal."

"It's not about the staying, it's about why you stayed. God, it's cold." Ben pulled his hands from his pockets, and crossed them, tucking his hands into his armpits. "You stayed for your family and friends. To keep them safe."

I nodded. "Yeah well," I shuffled my weight from one foot to the other. "Someone has too."

The quiet that followed that statement felt tense, punctuated only by the faint sounds of traffic rumbling past on the nearby main street.

It was Ben who finally broke the silence.

"I'm sorry about before, when I sprung all of that KissFerno stuff on you."

I waved him off. "Don't worry about it."

"No, it needs to be said." Glancing over at him, I found Ben staring down at his shoes as he continued. "I made a mistake on my profile, but I didn't pick up on it until much later. I wasn't cat-fishing you, or anything like that."

I raised an eyebrow when Ben finally raised his eyes to meet mine. "You don't need to explain yourself to me," I told him with all sincerity. "Online dating was how I first jumped into the gay scene years ago."

Ben shook his head fervently. "Seriously, I wasn't kidding before. I really am straight."

His voice sounded so sincere, that I really didn't know who Ben was trying to convince — myself or him.

If Ben was this deep in the closet, then I wasn't going to pry that door open. No matter how hot I thought he was.

'Damn it, Josh. Ben's strictly off limits as a hookup...no matter what his pretty eyes do to you.' I scolded myself. *'Arthur would kill me.'*

Besides, Ben would figure himself out in time, just like I did when I was in my mid twenties.

When I opened my mouth to assure Ben that I believed him, I was interrupted by the short sharp sound of a car horn. Turning towards the noise, I saw a cab roll to a stop outside the bar.

The cab driver leaned towards the opened passenger seat window of his vehicle. "I'm here to pickup Josh Wright?"

I nodded at the cab driver. "That's me," I answered, then twisted round to give Ben a mock-salute. "You and the old man get home safe, yah hear?"

Ben grinned, mirth coloring his eyes. "Goodnight, Josh"

And with that, I made my way into the cab, and relaxed back into the seat with an exhausted sigh.

Chapter 4

BEN

When the words on the page started to blur, I relented and finally took a break.

It was already well into the early evening, some eight hours after I'd started studying for the day.

But coursework waits for no-one. And my final year of pre-med was absolutely swamping me with it.

This weekend break from my college campus, was a chance to catchup with my folks, and go to my dad's retirement party. But, I still had too much work to get through. So, my stack of textbooks simply came along with me.

Shoving back the open textbook, I yawned as I rubbed away the dryness from my eyes. I was still feeling dehydrated from all the beer I'd drunk last night.

Sat at a small desk, in the guest room of my parents new home, I eased back into my chair and blew out a breath.

My parents had bought this house — downsizing our old family home — as soon as I'd left for college.

The house was modest, but still quaint, and it was situated on the edge of the Northside district. And it was the perfect place for my folks to live out their retirement years.

But, there wasn't a lot to do around here. And I didn't know any of the local neighbors.

On one hand, this distraction free environment meant that I could get caught up on a bunch of studying. But, it also meant there wasn't much to do if I needed to unwind afterwards.

My phone buzzed, startling me for a moment as it hummed atop the desk.

Picking up my phone, I was surprised to find a notification alerting me to a KissFerno message from *J-Heart3000*.

I unlocked my phone, and went straight into the dating app. But, at the last second I paused with my finger hovered over the 'read message' button.

I was really curious to see what Josh had sent. But, if I checked it, would that mean I was messing around with the guy?

Last night — after my dad and I finally left the bar — I made a promise to myself that I would delete my profile first thing in the morning.

But, as soon as I got back home, I went straight upstairs and collapsed onto the bed fast asleep. And the next morning I was so absorbed by my coursework, it had completely slipped my mind.

Until now.

'Still, Josh messaged me, not the other way around.' I thought to myself. *'It would be impolite not to at least read his message. Right?'*

And with that thought, I tapped open Josh's message.

 # J-Heart3000: Hey, B. Just reaching out to say sorry for the way I acted last night. I was a bit of an ass, didn't mean to push. Hope you are well. J

It took me a long moment to notice that I was wearing a broad smile on my face, as I reread Josh's message for a third time.

It felt strange, acting all giddy over another guy's simple apology.

But, despite his gruff demeanor towards me last night, there was something warm and inviting about the way Josh interacted with his crowd of friends at the party. And it made me want to get to know him better.

Or maybe I was simply feeling a little lonely — *and a lot bored* — and Josh messaging me was a great distraction.

So, setting all of my doubts aside, I opted to send Josh a message back.

B-Love2424: *Its ok, we r cool. I wd hv been pissed bout it 2. U get home safe?*

After tapping 'send', I placed my phone back onto the desk. And with a sigh I returned my attention back towards my textbook.

The words still blurred.

As I began to lightly slap my cheeks to re-energize myself, my phone buzzed again.

Picking my phone back up, to my mild shock, it was another message from Josh!

This time I didn't hesitate. It seemed like Josh was available for a quick messaging conversation. And I was more than happy to ignore my textbook, so that I could instead focus on Josh.

J-Heart3000: *Yes I did. Thanks for asking. And glad we are cool again. You should let me buy you another beer one day as a proper apology. You never got to finish the first one I gave you.*

Reading through the long message, I grinned. Seemed like Josh was much more chatty via text than in real-life.

That message was the longest string of words I'd gotten out of Josh since he found out I was B-Love2424.

I quickly typed in my reply.

B-Love2424: *Y not buy me that beer right now?*

I tapped 'send' before I stopped to think about it.

'Wait a second. Does that make me look like I'm coming onto him or something?' I hurriedly tapped out a followup message. I didn't want to give Josh the wrong idea.

B-Love2424: *I need a brk frm studying. Brain melting. Need to unwind. :) You'd b doing me a favor.*

I tapped the send button with a nod. *'That should clear things up. And if Josh doesn't reply back, well, then I could...'*

My train of thought was interrupted by the notification buzz going off.

 # J-Heart3000: I know a place. Send me your number and I'll text you the details.

Chapter 5

JOSH

For the third time in a row, Ben sank the black ball into the pocket in a single smooth long shot, winning the game.

"Yes!" Ben raised his hands triumphantly as I watched on bemused. Dropping his pool cue onto the table, he then made a show of taking a bow. "The cue-master reigns undefeated!"

I chuckled, placing my beer down on the edge of the pool table, and began an appreciative clap. "Well done."

"And...?" Ben cupped a hand around his ear as he tilted his head towards me as though encouraging me to speak up.

I rubbed my brow and sighed. "And the cue-master reigns undefeated..." I then rolled my eyes when Ben began to literally pat himself on the back. "...and who is clearly the most gracious opponent to ever play the game," I continued drolly.

Ben and I were in one of my favorite sports bars in the Eastside. And it was the first place that came to mind when Ben told me that he needed to unwind.

Other than the station, this place was pretty much my home away from home. It was a great place to relax after work, when I wanted to do something a little more than simply down a beer.

And right now, it was nice and quiet, with only a few patrons downing a few drinks, before the late-evening rush kicked in.

This place was neutral ground, and I never brought any of my hookups here.

And yet, (when Ben had arrived at the bar 30 minutes after I'd messaged him with the location), I felt a little bit excited. It felt silly, but I really wanted to impress Ben.

So, that is where my suggestion of a game of pool came in.

I'm not too modest to admit that I am a pretty decent pool player, easily beating all of the other guys back at the station. But, despite all the hours I'd put in at the pool table, Ben had trounced me three games in a row.

"If I'd known you were this good at pool, I would have picked a different game, like darts," I said as I jutted my chin over at the dartboard on the wall opposite. "Unless, of course, you're a crack shot at that too?" I wondered aloud.

Ben grinned. "Naw, pool is my hidden talent. I managed to pay for a lot of my textbooks betting against my friends at the pool table, in the college rec room."

"I don't doubt it," I said as I snagged my beer off the table, and stepped back to give Ben room to rack up another game.

Ben hummed in agreement. "I wasn't any good at football or athletics back in high school," Ben continued as he set about placing the pool balls into the rack. "Phys Ed wasn't my thing. But, once I got to college, I finally discovered my natural talent," Ben tapped his hand lightly on the green felt. "I find pool easier, because it's all about judging the angles, not cardio."

"With all of that college work, I'm surprised you've had the time to do anything else in your downtime," I said as I moved to pick up my pool cue. I then chuckled as I continued, "...other than making craft soda beers, of course."

Ben made a show of looking affronted, then cracked a smile. "You're never going to let that one go, are you." Ben then paused, thoughtfully tilting his head. "I needed an outlet to blow off steam, and pool works for me. Plus, I made a few bucks extra to help pay for all of my brewing ingredients. I guess you could say that pool helps me to make the *best* damn tasting beers in the world."

Ben stared pointedly at me with a single raised eyebrow, daring me to contradict him. But, I merely shrugged and raised my palms into the air in surrender.

"Sure, whatever you say." I grinned.

"Yeah, that's right." Ben returned my grin with a nod, and then grabbed his cue. He then strode around the table, and made his way over to the other end where I stood. "Pool is pretty much my third favorite thing to do in life...so the cue-master was born."

I shuffled back a couple steps to give Ben room to lean over the table and take his shot. It was then that I noticed Ben's firm jean-clad ass was right in my face.

It was firm, round, and altogether much too juicy for me to ignore. I tried to tear my eyes away from it, but I was transfixed.

'Damn,' I thought, when the sound of pool balls clacking finally woke me from my wet-daydream.

I quickly angled my eyes away as Ben turned around, and prayed that he hadn't noticed me leering. *'Damn it!'* I repeated the thought, cursing myself at almost having been caught.

My mind flashed with the image from Ben's dating app profile. Ben's face had been cropped out, but he'd hidden nothing of his naked torso, showing off his lean but well-defined muscle.

I clenched my jaw, and shook my head as though to shake away the memory of Ben's lickable abs.

Ben was straight, (or at least that's the story he was going with). Besides, he was Arthur's family. So, there was no chance I was going to try and hookup with him.

'Put that thought right out of your mind. Right Now!' I chastised myself.

"Hey? Josh?" Ben was waving a hand in my face, shaking me from my reverie. "You're up."

"Um, yup," I gave him a curt nod and quickly moved around him — careful not to brush up against his firm body — and then leaned down to take my shot.

And completely missed.

'Damn it,' I cursed myself again. My lusty thoughts of Ben had distracted me.

I seriously needed to get my mind off of this line of thinking. And that's when I remembered Ben's earlier divulgence. "What's your first thing?" I said as I moved out of the way to let Ben take his shot.

But, this time I was careful to keep his delicious ass out of my direct line of sight.

"Huh? First thing?" Ben took his shot smoothly, and the ball sunk right down into the pocket. And yet Ben was already moving around the table to get into position for his next shot.

I leaned against my cue as I watched the self-acclaimed cue-master work his magic once again.

"You said pool is your third favorite thing to do in your downtime," I clarified, shaking my head as Ben somehow managed to sink two pool balls off a single shot. "I'm guessing brewing beers is your favorite past-time?"

"Brewing? Naw. That's only second place," Ben answered as he hustled around the pool table again.

It took me a moment too long to realize that Ben was leaning over the table right in front of me. And it wasn't until my eyes again drifted down to his firm ass, that I remembered why I needed to keep a little distance.

Worse still, I could even feel my manhood begin to twitch with excitement at the sight of Ben leaning down over the table.

"So, what's the first thing?" I repeated, genuinely curious as to what Ben's answer would be.

As he straightened, Ben pivoted around to face me, but we were both now stood a little too close.

The corner spot of the bar — where the large pool table was — didn't really leave much room for us to maintain a respectable distance.

Ben fell silent as he carefully eyed me, and I noticed an unmistakable dilation of his pupils, and a touch of heat to his cheeks. And my eyes drifted down to find Ben's tongue sneaking out to wet his lips.

We stood like that for a long tense heated moment, and I could feel the front of my pants begin to tighten.

'Not now!' I thought as I hurriedly turned away. Quickly stepping around Ben, I cleared my throat while I tried to surreptitiously adjust my dick. But the brush of my hand, across the front of my pants, only made my cock stand to attention even more.

I needed to keep a bit of distance from Ben — just for a little bit — until I managed to calm my body down.

"Well, I guess coursework has to be your favorite thing right now." I tried to brush off the uncomfortable moment, angling my body slightly away from Ben who still stood stock still where I'd left him. He hadn't even turned round to face me as I spoke, but I continued talking anyway. "No choice, I suppose. That's simply the way it is when your studying something tough like medicine, right?" *Why was I rambling? What the hell was happening?* "Final year of pre-med must be tough."

Ben hummed a noncommittal sound as — with his back still towards me — he hustled around the table. It was strange to watch him awkwardly shuffle to the other side of the table like that. "Yeah it is," Ben answered, casting me an uncomfortable glance over his shoulder. "All of that studying. So tough. But, hey, are those bathrooms?" Ben rushed out the words. Confused, I wordlessly watched as he paced off in the direction of the nearest bathroom. "I'll be right back."

And with that, Ben was gone.

To Be Continued...

To read the rest of 'Hard Wright' you can purchase it right now by visiting here: https://books2read.com/u/38WrPw

ABOUT THE AUTHOR

Author B.T. Haiyes loves romance books, espresso and cheesecake — in no particular order.

Having started her freelance writing career back in 2015, she now carves out time in her work schedule, to write the kind of stories she loves to read.

Stories about men finding love in the most unlikely of places, are her particular favorites. Which is why she writes so much heartfelt MM insta-love short story fiction.

In her spare time — when she isn't writing or reading — she also likes to knit, cycle, and hike nearby trails.

www.ingramcontent.com/pod-product-compliance
Lightning Source LLC
Chambersburg PA
CBHW061710130726

47996CB00006B/2237